Fish
is
Fish

Fish
is
Fish

Alfred A. Knopf, New York

At the edge of the woods there was a pond, and there a minnow and a tadpole swam among the weeds. They were inseparable friends.

One morning the tadpole discovered that during the night he had grown two little legs.

"Look," he said triumphantly. "Look, I am a frog!"

"Nonsense," said the minnow. "How could you be a frog if only last night you were a little fish, just like me!"

They argued and argued until finally the tadpole said, "Frogs are frogs and fish is fish and that's that!"

In the weeks that followed, the tadpole grew tiny front legs and
his tail got smaller and smaller.

And then one fine day, a real frog now, he climbed out of the water and onto the grassy bank.

The minnow too had grown and had become a full-fledged fish.
He often wondered where his four-footed friend had gone. But
days and weeks went by and the frog did not return.

Then one day, with a happy splash that shook the weeds, the frog jumped into the pond.

"Where have you been?" asked the fish excitedly.

"I have been about the world—hopping here and there," said the frog, "and I have seen extraordinary things."

"Like what?" asked the fish.

"Birds," said the frog mysteriously. "Birds!" And he told the fish about the birds, who had wings, and two legs, and many, many colors.

As the frog talked, his friend saw the birds fly through his mind like large feathered fish.

"What else?" asked the fish impatiently.

"Cows," said the frog. "Cows! They have four legs, horns, eat grass, and carry pink bags of milk."

"And people!" said the frog. "Men, women, children!" And he talked and talked until it was dark in the pond.

But the picture in the fish's mind was full of lights and colors and marvelous things and he couldn't sleep. Ah, if he could only jump about like his friend and see that wonderful world.

And so the days went by. The frog had gone and the fish just lay there dreaming about birds in flight, grazing cows, and those strange animals, all dressed up, that his friend called people.

One day he finally decided that come what may, he too must see them. And so with a mighty whack of the tail he jumped clear out of the water onto the bank.

He landed in the dry, warm grass and there he lay gasping for air, unable to breathe or to move. "Help," he groaned feebly.

Luckily the frog, who had been hunting butterflies nearby, saw him and with all his strength pushed him back into the pond.

Still stunned, the fish floated about for an instant. Then he breathed deeply, letting the clean cool water run through his gills. Now he felt weightless again and with an ever-so-slight motion of the tail he could move to and fro, up and down, as before.

   The sunrays reached down within the weeds and gently shifted patches of luminous color. This world was surely the most beautiful of all worlds. He smiled at his friend the frog, who sat watching him from a lily leaf. "You were right," he said. "Fish is fish."

THIS IS A BORZOI BOOK PUBLISHED BY ALFRED A. KNOPF

Copyright © 1970 by Leo Lionni. Copyright renewed 1998 by Leo Lionni.

All rights reserved under International and Pan-American Copyright Conventions. Published in the

United States by Alfred A. Knopf, an imprint of Random House Children's Books, a division of Random

House, Inc., New York, and simultaneously in Canada by Random House of Canada Limited, Toronto.

Distributed by Random House, Inc., New York.

KNOPF, BORZOI BOOKS, and the colophon are registered trademarks of Random House, Inc.

www.randomhouse.com/kids

Library of Congress Cataloging-in-Publication Data

Lionni, Leo, 1910–1999. / Fish is fish.

p. cm.

78-117452

ISBN 0-394-80440-6 (trade) 20 19 18 17 16 15

ISBN 0-394-90440-0 (lib. bdg.) 20 19 18 17 16

MANUFACTURED IN MALAYSIA

January 2005